P9-DZX-763
This book belongs to:
Korrey
Eric
King
GLUE
10
MB
MB

Published by Grolier Direct Marketing, Danbury, Connecticut

Printed in the U.S.A.

ISBN 0-7172-8273-2

by Michaela Muntean illustrated by Tom Cooke

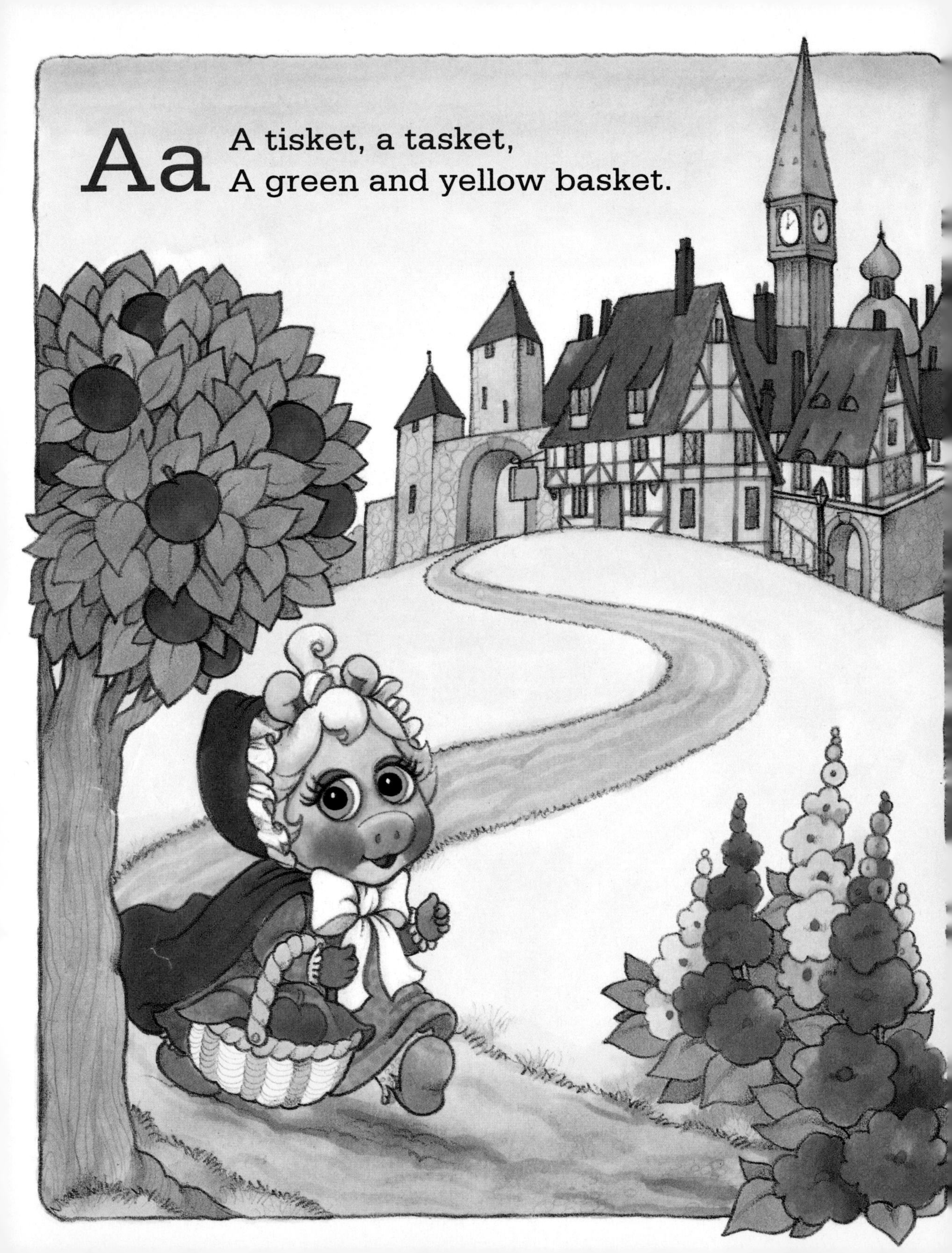
Aa A tisket, a tasket,
A green and yellow basket.

Bb

Baa, baa, black sheep, have you any wool?
Yes sir, yes sir, three bags full.

Cc

Cobbler, cobbler, mend my shoe.
Get it done by half past two.

Dd Diddle, diddle, dumpling, my son John,
Went to bed with his stockings on.

Ee Eeny, meeny, miney, moe,
Catch a tiger by the toe.

Ff Flying man, flying man, up in the sky,
Where are you going to, flying so high?

Gg Georgie Porgie, pudding and pie,
Kissed the girls and made them cry.

Hh Humpty Dumpty sat on a wall,
Humpty Dumpty had a great fall.

Ii Itsy-bitsy spider crawled up the waterspout.
Down came the rain and washed the spider out.

Jj
Jack and Jill went up the hill
To fetch a pail of water.

Kk Kitty and I, Kitty and me,
We like to sleep till half past three.

Ll Little Boy Blue, come blow your horn,
The sheep's in the meadow,
the cow's in the corn.

Mm Mary, Mary, quite contrary,
How does your garden grow?

Nn Needles and pins, needles and pins,
When you drop the first stitch,
the trouble begins.

Oo
Old King Cole was a merry old soul,
And a merry old soul was he.

Pp Pease porridge hot, pease porridge cold,
Pease porridge in the pot, nine days old.

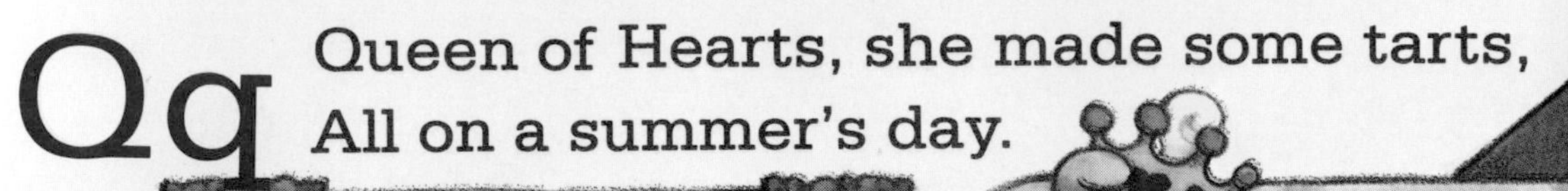

Qq Queen of Hearts, she made some tarts,
All on a summer's day.

Rr Ring around the rosie, a pocket full of posie,
Ashes, ashes, all fall down.

Ss Sing a song of sixpence, a pocket full of rye,
Four-and-twenty blackbirds baked in a pie.

Tt Twinkle, twinkle, little star,
How I wonder what you are.

Uu Upsy-daisy, over and 'round,
Touch the sky, then touch the ground.

Vv Violets in the valley,
Tulips on the hill,
I know they've always grown there;
I think they always will.

Ww Wee Willie Winkie
runs through the town,
Upstairs and downstairs,
in his nightgown.

Xx X marks the spot — or perhaps it does not.
I tried to remember, but then I forgot.

Yy Yankee Doodle went to town,
Riding on a pony.

Zz Zachary Thackery stays up all night.
Zachary Thackery, blow out the light!

A
DOG